To the memory of
MARGARET RINALDI LA MARE,
good egg, great friend
—R.J.

To my dad
—J.D.

Tessa Takes Wing

Richard Jackson   Pictures by Julie Downing

A NEAL PORTER BOOK

ROARING BROOK PRESS

NEW YORK

Text copyright © 2018 by Richard Jackson
Illustrations copyright © 2018 by Julie Downing
A Neal Porter Book
Published by Roaring Brook Press
Roaring Brook Press is a division of Holtzbrinck Publishing Holdings Limited Partnership
175 Fifth Avenue, New York, NY 10010
The art for this book was created using watercolor and colored pencil and combined digitally.
mackids.com

Library of Congress Control Number: 2017957302
ISBN: 978-1-62672-439-6

Our books may be purchased in bulk for promotional, educational, or business use. Please
contact your local bookseller or the Macmillan Corporate and Premium Sales Department
at (800) 221-7945 ext.5442 or by e-mail at MacmillanSpecialMarkets@macmillan.com

First edition, 2018
Book design by Jennifer Browne
Printed in China by Toppan Leefung Printing Ltd., Dongguan City, Guangdong Province

1 3 5 7 9 10 8 6 4 2

"Up," Tessa says to no one.

No one answers.

Goody, she thinks and jumps up herself . . .

and up . . .

and out of her crib . . .

and up . . .

and up . . .

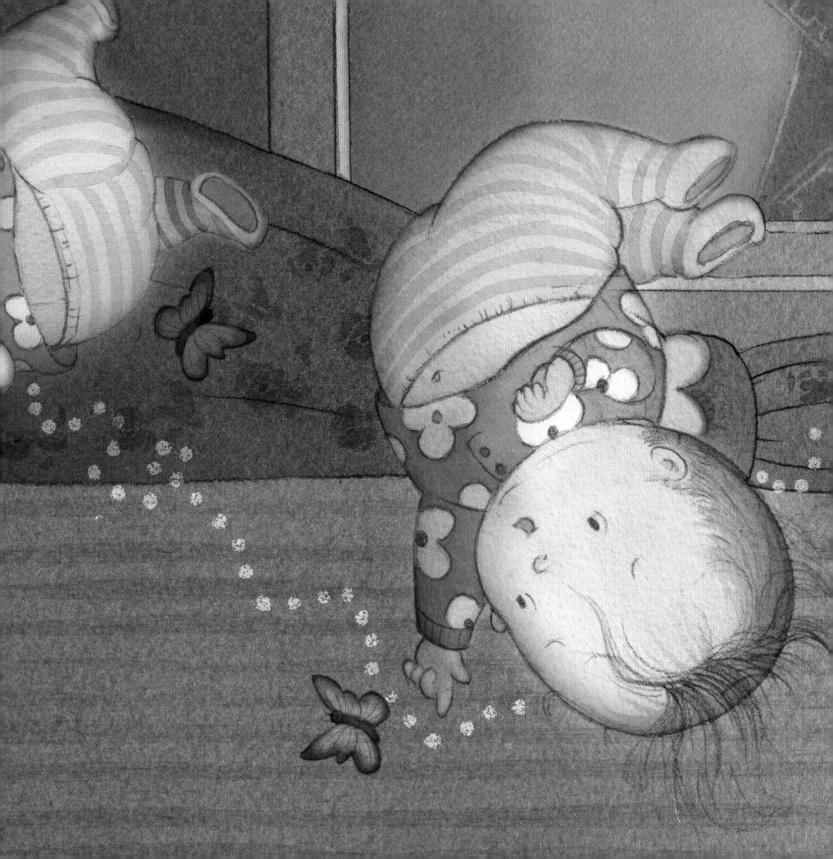

higher even
than yesterday!

No one sees
Tessa hug Maggie's
blue elephant . . .

drive her fire truck . . .

spin her polka-dotted
umbrella . . .

then open a book . . .

and another . . .

and another.

Outside, the dawn light—
up now with Tessa—
makes reading easier.

Bingo follows her finger,
with one eye open.

Good Bingo, she thinks.
Good dog.

Keeping quiet . . .

. . . except for his tail.
Thump, thump!
Thump!

Uh-oh, Bingo.
Daddy will hear.

Quick!

A flick,

a flutter,

and Tessa
is up . . .

up . . .

and back
to her crib.
So close!
Bingo yawns.
Maggie stirs.

Daddy whispers
at the door,
"Hello,
Honeybee—
you're up
early."

"Up," Tessa says.

Daddy lifts her
up, up—
higher even than
yesterday.

And soon
everyone is up—
to see Tessa . . .

up in her
high chair . . .

up on Daddy's
shoulders . . .

up, up high
in Mama's arms—
almost as if she
were flying—

almost—

until naptime.